My Little Friend®

GOES TO A BASEBALL GAME

By Evelyn M. Finnegan

Illustrations by Diane R. Houghton

LITTLE FRIEND PRESS

SCITUATE, MASSACHUSETTS

First U.S. edition 1994.
Printed in China. Published
in the United States
by Little Friend Press,
Scituate, Massachusetts.

ISBN 0-9641285-0-0

Library of Congress
Catalog Card Number: 94-96099

Second Printing

LITTLE FRIEND PRESS
28 NEW DRIFTWAY
SCITUATE, MASSACHUSETTS 02066

To my son Peter who believes.

To my grandson Paul who is our inspiration.

What a beautiful
spring morning!

The sun is just
rising, its golden
light coming through
my bedroom window.

Today is a special
day because . . .

My Little Friend and I are going to the
ballpark with my mother and father.

We are both very excited because
this is the first time we have ever
gone to a baseball game.

Time to wake up My Little Friend and
get ready for the trip to the big city.

"Wake up My Little Friend!"

My mom said it won't be very cold today
so I can wear my new blue sweater that
Nana made especially for me.

"Come, jump inside your secret pocket,
My Little Friend."

"Good morning Mom and Dad!
Mmmmmmmmm . . .
breakfast looks really good."

My Little Friend doesn't need
to have breakfast but he wants me
to eat because it's good for me.

Now it's time for all of us to take the long drive into the city.

My dad buckles my seat belt so I will be safe.

Along the way we pass several animals . . .

There is a brown horse and a black and white cow.

11

My Little Friend and I begin to see
tall buildings as we enter the big city.

It's good My Little Friend is safe
in his secret pocket.

My dad parks the car and we all
hold hands so we won't get
separated as we enter the ballpark.

The man with the red hat takes our
tickets . . . My Little Friend doesn't
need a ticket because he is with me.

15

Wow, look at all the people in the
ballpark! My Little Friend and
I have never seen so many people.

We all sit together . . .

My Little Friend and I are safe and
sound between my parents.

Here comes a man yelling something . . .
He is carrying many brown bags.

"What is he carrying?" My Little Friend asks.

"Get Your Peanuts!"

My dad passes some money to the peanut man
and he throws three bags of peanuts to us.

One bag falls under my seat. I lean over to pick it up.

The baseball game is very exciting.
We are busy watching and cheering!

As we get ready to leave our seats I look
to see how My Little Friend is doing . . .

Oh no! Where is My Little Friend?
He should be in his secret pocket.

"Mom . . . have you seen My Little Friend?"
"No dear, I haven't."

"Dad . . . have you seen My Little Friend?"
"No Paul, I haven't. Are you sure you
brought him along today?"

"Oh yes, he is always with me!"

I have to find My Little Friend!

My mom and dad look all around
and I check under my seat.

I really miss My Little Friend.

Where could he be?

Suddenly . . . a man in front of us shouts "Who is this in my peanuts?"

And he holds up My Little Friend.

I'm so happy now that I've
found My Little Friend.

I hold him tightly in my hands.

My mom says not to worry because
she will make a seat belt for my
secret pocket so I will always have
My Little Friend with me.

31

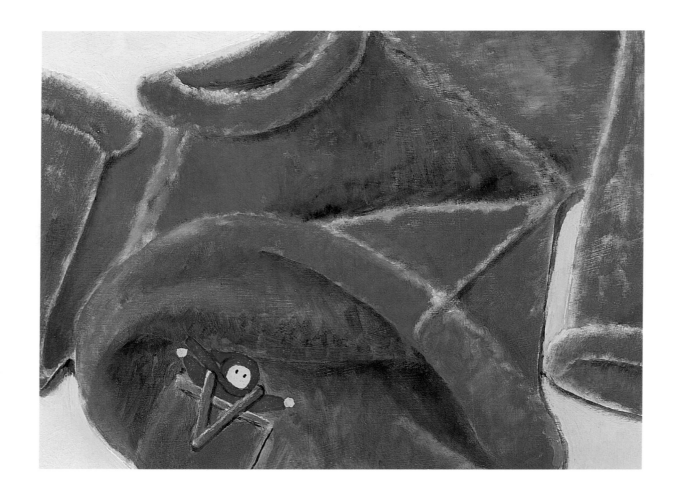

The End.

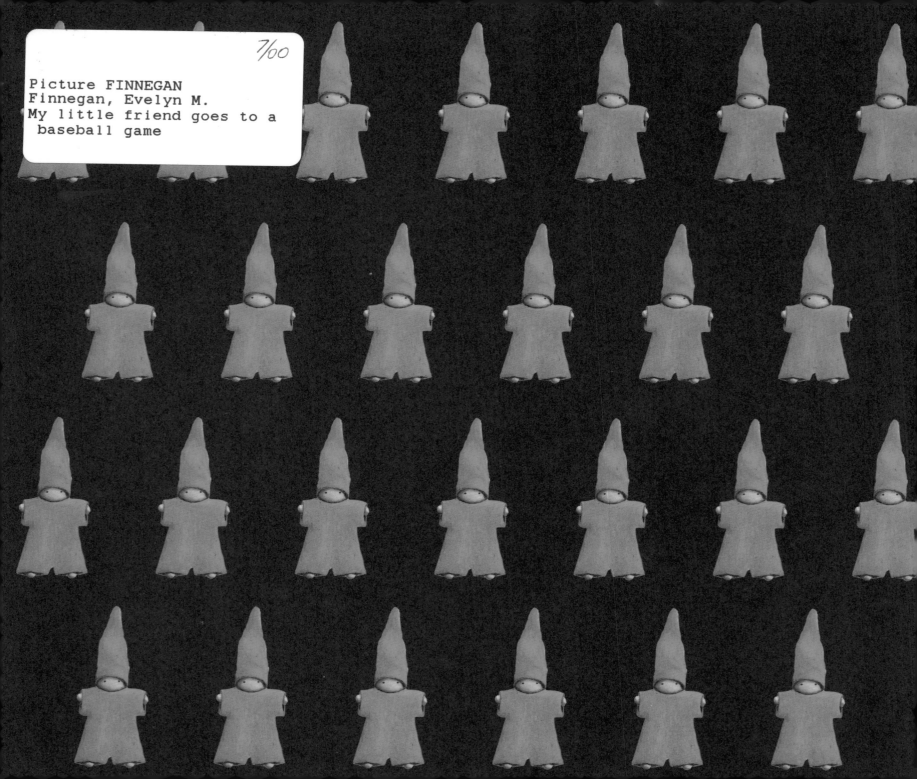